Black Cat

S.M. FLANAGAN

This edition first published in paperback by
Michael Terence Publishing in 2023
www.mtp.agency

Copyright © 2023 S.M. Flanagan

S.M. Flanagan has asserted the right to be identified as
the author of this work in accordance with the
Copyright, Designs and Patents Act 1988

ISBN 9781800945395

No part of this publication may be reproduced, stored
in a retrieval system, or transmitted, in any form or
by any means, electronic, mechanical, photocopying,
recording or otherwise, without the prior
permission of the publisher

Cover image
Copyright © Nikolay2
www.123rf.com

Cover design
Copyright © 2023 Michael Terence Publishing

Dedication

This book is dedicated to the remembrance of our closed-down R C College which stays deep in our memories.

Contents

Introduction 1

1: Stella's Chess Demonstration 2

2: Mark Listened to Stella Sing 8

3: Mark Attended a Seminar 13

4: Backslide 16

5: Drinking 18

6: Mark's Life Changes 21

7: Mark's Last Moments (with a Catholic Schoolgirl) 24

8: Stella's Birthday 26

9: Last Memory 28

10: Mark's Profound Vision 29

Introduction

Remembering a black cat one night at midnight. A witch's cat. Was it an omen? Was it something frightening? A mystic symbolism!

At that time of midnight Mark remained unafraid since he been a regular churchgoer. Mark's fate changed since he backslid. He cherished the thing he dearly loved and treasured. He made a sacrifice!

His deep spirituality remained a mystery!

1
Stella's Chess Demonstration

Stella and her Mother came around to Mrs Tomkins' house. Mark Tomkins the son greeted Stella, a Fourth-Year schoolgirl. Stella looked rather beautiful dressed in her school uniform. (It was a nicer lovelier one.)

Mark stayed with Stella downstairs in the dining room while Mrs Tomkins and Mrs Avery went upstairs together. Both friends were amiable.

Stella moved the forelock away from her eyes. Stella sat down at the dining table. Looking at the chess set in front of her. The chess pieces were carved from wood.

Mark stood still and watched Stella move chess pieces around the chess board. Stella concentrated on moving every chessman.

With wonder Mark looked at Stella demonstrating every chess piece's move. Stella moved every chess piece well. Keeping cool and calm while demonstrating every chess piece's move. Stella impressed Mark with her impressive knowledge of playing chess.

"Now the Bishop moves diagonally. It moves only on its diagonal colour. It is powerful. Two Bishops combined are very powerful on their flanks. They can pin down too. The Rook is called the Castle. It is a defensive chess piece. It is used later in a chess game for offensive, counter-attack and to make an attack. It is an attacking and defensive chess piece. It only moves horizontally. Two Rooks combined are deadly on an empty board. Usually in games a player has only one Castle. The Rook is a defensive chess piece. It is used in defence to Castle. Now the Knight is an effective and impressive chess piece. It moves in an 'L' shape and can fork chessmen. It is an admirable and efficient chess piece. It is both good in defence and attack. The Knight jumps over. The Queen is the most powerful chess piece. It moves diagonally and horizontally. The usual tendency is that the player tends to depend too much on the Queen. Once the Queen is taken the game changes. The player has to depend on other chess pieces. Usually the Rooks, Knights and Bishops. Of course, a player can be weaker without their Queen and be exposed. The player has to play well by using the other pieces effectively.

"Sometimes chess games are lost when the player's Queen is taken. The game is one-sided. Now the Pawn can move one square or two squares. It can do en passant too. The Pawns is a defensive chess piece. The Foot Soldier is good and rather too powerful in Pawn formation. A Pawn is very useful and effective at the end of a chess game. When a Pawn reaches the other side of a chessboard it can then be converted into a Queen! What a transformation! That makes all the difference in chess games.

"Last but not least, the King moves only one square. It is easily attacked and checkmated.

"Checkmates can occur when the King is unprotected, exposed and defenceless. Stalemates can occur seldom in games. The King has to be defended and protected at all times by its Pawns and Rooks. If the King is under attack, it is exposed and vulnerable. It is susceptible to attack and "check." Once the King has been checkmated, finally the game is over. Players can also resign too.

"I do wonder what the implication of that means in chess," said Stella articulately.

Mark was impressed at Stella's knowledge of chess. He admired the good chess player.

"I am impressed. You have demonstrated that well. It is a good demonstration," said Mark admiringly.

Stella insisted Mark should keep on playing chess. She encouraged him.

"Whatever you do, don't give up on chess."

"I will try. I don't have anyone to play with," said Mark unconfidently.

"You must keep playing chess. I can't stress enough the importance of it," emphasised Stella.

"Regarding chess. Where are you at with it?" enquired Mark.

Stella reflected on how she'd won and lost games. "I am winning and losing. Hopefully I am winning more games than I am losing!"

"How is your brother?" asked Mark.

"Morgan is fine. He's leaving school this year," replied Stella.

"Oh! What a pity. Morgan likes school, doesn't he?" murmured Mark.

"I don't know. I have to ask him," grinned Stella.

Suddenly Mrs Avery and Mark's Mother came downstairs. They both entered the dining room. The door was ajar. Overhearing them speak, Mrs Tomkins interrupted.

"My son is a bachelor. He has never married," said Mother concernedly.

The son remained unashamed of being unmarried.

"I am single. I never took up the offer of marriage. I am still unmarried," blushed Mark.

Stella shook her hair. She made a gesture. A schoolgirl's charm.

"You haven't got a son or daughter?" remarked Stella.

"No. I haven't tied the knot yet. Is that wrong?" said Mark unashamedly.

"No. It's not wrong."

"My son is single. A Bachelor," said Mother ashamedly.

With curiosity, Stella wondered. Stella was inquisitive.

"Mark, what were your schooldays like? Tell me. I would like to know," asked Stella.

With impatience Mrs Avery forced her daughter to leave.

"Stella, we haven't time," said Mother impatiently.

"Mark, tell me. I would really like to know," insisted Stella.

Mark pressed for an answer, replied,

"I went to a good Grammar. I had a fair education. I could have done a lot better than I did," regretted Mark.

"That school of yours no longer exists," muttered Stella.

Mark explained himself.

"It doesn't. My Grammar closed down. I believe that a new one has opened up elsewhere. It is established."

"Oh, that is a shame," mumbled Stella.

Mrs Tomkins got confused by the institutional differences of new-founded institutes.

"My son went to a secondary modern. He did not do well," blurted out Mother.

"You're bright. You must do well at school. Don't waste your time," insisted Mark.

"My parents don't tolerate me as I slack. They insist I am educated. That I have a good education. It's interesting. What other things can you tell me?" wondered Stella.

Mark whispered, realising he was blurting out and had no wish to blab out anything else. He was aware of them listening and paying attention to him. Mark pressed a finger against his lips. He insisted on keeping quiet about it.

"When you are older, I will tell you."

Moving towards Stella. Stepping closer. Mark put his hand on Stella's shoulder. He patted her affectionately. A gentle touch.

Standing, Stella smiled at Mark with joyful delight. The intelligent schoolgirl favoured Mark. Stella always looked forward to coming around to Mark's parents' house. Stella and her Mother were good friends of Mark's Mother.

Mark showed Stella and her Mother and his parent out of the house.

Going back indoors, Mark slumped in the armchair and nodded off. He took comfort from being comfortable.

2
Mark Listened to Stella Sing

Mrs Tomkins and Mrs Avery went upstairs together while Mark and Stella stayed together in the lounge where they both had a nice mug of tea. They were refreshed from drinking their refreshing tea. The caffeine was a stimulant. They nibbled on a biscuit each.

Both Mark and Stella enjoyed each other's company. Being together once again in their presence. It remained such a joyful pleasure. The experienced Librarian and the sophisticated schoolgirl talked. Stella wanted to talk about something topical. A reminder. A topic which Stella reminded Mark of when she was last interrupted by her Mother when leaving together on their previous visit to Mrs Tomkins' house.

Stella acted in a way of course that was fitting, which was studious and remindful. She had a book on her lap. Her lovely shapely legs showing her beautiful plain black stockings. She caressed her leg. The material of her stocking.

"Now we're alone, why don't you tell me about your schooldays?" insisted Stella.

"What is there to tell?" said Mark unenthusiastically.

"Go on! Tell me about your schooldays," prompted Stella repeatedly.

"My time at Grammar was disappointing. I just didn't do as well as I ought to have done. The others did far better than me. I should have done better. I can't forget my schooldays. They still do mean the world to me. They say school is the best days of one's life. Well, is it? It must be true. There must be some truth in it," said Mark honestly.

"I have heard of that saying. I guess it's true. It does have a truthful meaning. It's quite profound," responded Stella.

"How is school?" asked Mark.

"Oh! It is tough. I am getting through it," replied Stella.

"How is music?" asked Mark.

"I like music. I am not a violin player. I am better at singing," said Stella modestly.

"Why don't you stick to singing? Isn't that the better thing to do? Why don't you sing to me?"

Getting up and standing still. Stella was surprised at Mark's request for her to sing. Without any anticipation she was unprepared.

"What?" said Stella murmuringly.

"Anything," insisted Mark.

Stella took a deep breath. She breathed. She stood up and preened herself.

"Well here goes."

With confidence Stella sang well. It certainly surprised her how well she sang.

DAWN

LOVE ME TO DAWN
MY DAWN LOVE
LOVE ME TO DAWN
STAY WITH ME
MY LOVE
STAY WITH ME TO DAWN.

I AM WITH YOU TO DAWN
TO THE REST OF DAWN
WITH YOU TILL THE REST OF DAWN
MY LOVE
WITH US TOGETHER AT DAWN

Mark clapped his hands. He was impressed by her good voice. At how well Stella sang. He admired her sweet voice. It sounded breathy.

"Did you like it?"

"Yeah. Loved it," replied Mark.

Mrs Tomkins and Mrs Avery entered the lounge. Stella and Mark followed them out of the lounge. Mark showed Mrs Avery and her daughter and his Mother out of the detached house. Mark stayed indoors. All alone by himself in the house.

One Sunday evening Mark went to church. A Sunday Service.

At the end of the church service a friendly churchgoer sitting next to him took the opportunity to talk to him. The middle-aged lady recommended that he should go to YP. Mark took the offer of the invitation and decided to go.

Mark attended YP one Friday night.

When coming back home from YP very late at night, Mark accompanied an acquaintance back to his house where he lived in a residential neighbourhood. Suddenly along the pavement near the road Mark found a beautiful black cat with brilliant green eyes and shiny black fur with a long tail, roaming in the night at midnight.

At that time Mark was unafraid with no fearful superstitions. He wasn't superstitious at all. At a residential road, Mark left the acquaintance. Going back to his home in the moonlit night. He lived a few roads away from that acquaintance of his. (Mark had been acquainted with the acquaintance's father.)

The Repast

From being warmly invited to an acquaintance's house. There he joined others for a repast in the garden. It was a nice treat. A most welcoming invitation.

At that time Mark unappreciated the treat. He was ungrateful and unthoughtful and selfish.

Looking back, he had a pleasant time.

An Invitation from an Acquaintance

The thoughtful acquaintance invited Mark to his Tudor-style house.

Mark stayed there a short time and talked. Today it was a brief visit which happened a long time ago. One which he unremembered and forgot. Years and years ago. Mark thought they were unusually strange. He was ignorant of them that they practiced Judaism. Without any knowledge, it was a religious ignorance.

3

Mark Attended a Seminar

At this time Mark had gone to a Bible week for only a day. This scenic location was in beautiful countryside.

Mark went with a friend to attend a seminar that afternoon. At this particular seminar the speaker talked about temptation. The drawback of it. How a Christian can resist temptation by one's Christian's faith. That resisting temptation remains the most important factor in a Christian's life and their deep spirituality!

The pastor talked about passages from scriptures. He quoted them. From the Old Testament.

Mark wondered about temptation. It did not seem apparent to his life. What's the implication of temptation? How is this relevant today in society and one's life?

The pastor also talked about common addictions, addicted sufferers! How one's faith was restored and their health was back to normal!

Due to Mark being ordinary and downright mediocre as well as discontented, he did not believe in Christianity. He was still an unbeliever of the Christian faith.

At this seminar. A disturbing one! He stayed till the very end of it in a big marquee. The setting was romantic. An over-excited Mark had exciting fantasies and dreams of a delirious romance!

Mark's experience of this was quite different, strange and unusual from anything else he had experienced.

Leaving the fields, he came across sexy desirable young women whom he desired. They all unnoticed him. Taking no notice of him. From their first impressions they found him unappealing and undesirable.

Mark was humiliated, miserable, unhappy and disappointed.

Leaving the lovely field with a friend he left to get driven back home. The frenzied passenger awaited this arrangement which been organised. Their departure from a seminar (at a bible week) rather too late in the day.

After the long journey home. Mark reached home. Entering indoors. Going inside a room. There he met his Mother waiting for him.

"How was it?" asked Mother.

Mark was unsophisticated and sceptical as he made a comment and passed judgement.

"I didn't really make much of an impression on anyone, no-one took any notice of me. A moron! Today in actual fact I felt quite insignificant. All this religious lark!" said Mark sceptically.

"Son. Don't doubt. Believe!"

"I can't. I don't believe," admitted Son.

4

Backslide

Going to church several times, Mark hoped to see a woman whom he fancied and desired. A fanciful besotted obsessiveness for her. It wasn't because of faith but of constant obsession and infatuation. An obsessive desire and obsessional pursuit of a desirable lovely woman. No longer finding her at church anymore. Mark ended up at being a backslider! Backsliding yet again!

At that age Mark was confused, wayward, wild, stubborn and set in his ways. For only a few weeks he also attended home groups every Thursday night. He soon backslid, turning back to his usual ways. He regressed. Mark sinned as usual. Sinning was a norm in his life! He reverted to his sinful ways.

Mark watched sex and horror on television and videos. He lied and stole. A thief, he was a drinker and overindulgent. Life for him was increasingly becoming sin. He lost his faith in God. He backslid! A bad sinner!

He lived a life of sin. His life becoming darkness. He lied, stole and cheated. He became depraved, corrupted and debauched (not quite a debauchee yet).

Mark's Mother was corrupt and wanton. He followed suit like his nasty Mother. It seemed to run in the family. He hated his Mother. His Mother ill-treated and neglected him. He was deprived. His Father abandoned and deserted him when he was only a teenager. A teenage schoolboy who started secondary school. At the start of the Autumn Term.

Coming out of his house to go to a supermarket. Within walking distance. He shopped. He bought groceries. As he came back to get home. When crossing a busy road. A car speeding almost ran him over. Mark was almost a casualty. He was nearly knocked over!

His plastic bag split as a result of it. He was almost killed, run over!

Getting back home. He was lucky to have survived. He was relieved to still be alive. He locked himself in his bedroom. He reflected on it. With fear, apprehension and anxiety he shook. He stayed in his bedroom. He must have lost a life! One at least!

He remained badly shaken. He soon recovered from his bad shock.

He stayed in the next day. Not really having a will to go out whatsoever. Literally Mark was still having a deep fear of the unexpected.

5

Drinking

Standing by the window as he slouched. Mark reflected on a memory of his in the past. With a deep contemplation he reflected on it.

On one hot summer day Mark went to a park with a pretentious friend. Denny's airs and graces were a false pretence. Sitting on a hilly slope Mark and Denny shared a bottle of dry wine together. They both indulged in drinking. A binge.

At that time Mark was inclined to suicide. He had a suicidal tendency. Mark became sad, bereaved, mournful and miserable. (Mark backslid. He lost his faith.)

Regarding his sexuality, sexual behaviour, matters and conduct, Mark still remained a prude, decent, straitlaced and prudish.

Today Mark was idle and lazy being alone with his so-called friend in a park. A layabout and unemployed.

Mark knew Denny was such a bad influence. He too was unemployed. Denny's prospects were bleak. Denny a pretentious layabout did actually appear to be somewhat spiritual and philosophical. He seemed to be quite knowledgeable about the scriptures. Mark a backslider who had completely lost his faith. His scriptural foundation of the word. The fundamental basis of the basic scriptures.

A few weeks later when going to a park with his so-called friends. He spent only a short time with them. With them leaving the park Denny and Nik climbed over the iron railings. Mark tried to climb over as well. As he tried to jump down, a spike of an iron railing caught the hem of his jeans and ripped it. Mark almost fell headlong and was left hanging. He almost had concussion. A bad accident!

Mark nearly bumped his head against an iron railing due to impact. A Samaritan took hold of him, his body dangling. He lifted him up. He disentangled a hem caught on a spike of an iron railing. The Samaritan took him down and lowered him gently back down onto his feet.

Mark was bewildered, shocked and dazed. This may well be two lives lost already.

On the streets two vandals were vandalising. Mark was uninvolved in it.

Later that same day on a bus one of them made fun of a passenger because of his skin colour and ethnicity.

Mark was sitting in a row at the back of the bus. The thug got up from his seat. He beat up the two delinquents. Mark escaped. He was deeply shocked by his ordeal. Perhaps another of his lives lost!

That made the grand total of four lives lost!

6

Mark's Life Changes

Mark becoming suicidal had attempted suicide, with suicide attempts. He lost the will to live. He recovered from his suicide attempts. Mark felt lonely, miserable and deeply unhappy. He was also rejected, abandoned and deserted. From time to time his Mother encouraged her son to read the scriptures. So, he would allocate time to read his bible every day. He got in the habit of reading his bible. He began to believe in the word. Then he would pray afterwards. The believer prayed. He was prayerful and deeply contemplative.

Mark become converted to a Christian! The repenter repented of his sins committed. He sought salvation and also redemption. His life became better. Things improved for him. He now cherished silence, peace and quietude. Nowadays there weren't any disturbances. But quietude and great peace in his life. He was pacified by solitude and quietness. He relished the peace and silence in his life at times.

Mark turned to the Lord. His life miraculously transformed. He applied for a post. Luckily at a Library the Applicant got a job working as a Librarian's Assistant at the Bibliographical Department.

Today late in the afternoon Mark spent precious time with Stella, a lovely schoolgirl. He knew his time was running out with her. In the luxurious lounge Mark sat down with Stella. Mrs Avery stayed with his Mother in the kitchen. Mark felt regenerated, ebullient and joyful at being in the presence of Stella, a happy and cheerful schoolgirl.

"When you are older. You will forget me. You will have your own life to live," said Mark.

"Hey! I don't forget you. How can I. You will still be in my memory," admitted Stella.

Mark admired Stella. A virtuous Catholic schoolgirl. Looking beautiful.

"Your life is your own. You will stop seeing me. Won't you? And you'll be doing your other things," predicted Mark.

"I will still see you. And your Mother, of course. Why should things be any different?"

Mark gazed at the elegant, stunningly lovely schoolgirl. He admired her stunning, natural girlish look. Her suntanned cheeks were aglow and flushed and her fair complexion also ruddy – and peachy too. Stella sat with grace. Stella's poise was natural. Stella was sitting gracefully with her legs crossed and arms folded. With a joyful expression.

"Do you think school is the best days of one's life?" wondered Mark.

"That's not so hard. I guess. I do believe it is. There must be some truth in it. When I get older, I will relive my experience. I will tell the tale," said Stella candidly.

Mark's memory of Stella a virgin was a beautiful one. Nothing else could compare to it or anything else in his life.

Stella didn't talk about being a Head Girl or a Prefect. She kept it confidential, private and personal. She did not want to brag about it (or her achievements). As the stress and seriousness of it was too much to bear and endure at lunch times at college.

Mark stayed with Stella until she and her Mother went home.

Mark did not see Stella and Mrs Avery until about a fortnight later.

At present Mark was unafraid of darkness. He never did see a black cat again. Or did he? A confusion of mysticism!

He remembered a black cat he once saw at midnight. An omen!

Mark saw the light. There in direct sunlight he saw beautiful virgins in the light. Was it reminiscent of a girls' maypole dance? A virgins'!

Mark valued and treasured a shrine too. Of course, anything like it. Mark treated things in a shrine-like way. It may have been an objective of his! It's an objectival perception! Mark had a virtue. The virgins too were one of them in his visions.

7

Mark's Last Moments (with a Catholic Schoolgirl)

Mrs Avery and her pretty daughter with sandy hair came to visit Mark's Mother. Their visit was a short one. During that time Mrs Avery spent time with his Mother in the kitchen while Mark stayed with Stella in the study. He took the time to put the Encyclopaedias he had taken out, back on the shelves of the cabinet.

"Today is my last day at school. I am a school leaver," mentioned Stella tearfully.

"Oh! Is it. I am sad to see you leave. I have got attached to you. Seeing you dressed like this," stared Mark.

"You will still see me. My Mother and me are friends of your Mother," assured Stella.

"Oh! Good! Are you going back to school next term?"

"No. I will be going to college," answered Stella.

"Oh, that is a shame. I won't see you like this again," gasped Mark.

"It's a pity. I am sad myself. It's time to move on," sighed Stella.

Mark stood up straight. He took a final glimpse of Stella's finely lovely school uniform. Her black stockings a breath-taking loveliness on her beautiful shapely legs.

Mark overwhelmed by the sight of it had admired and marvelled at it.

"Things will change. You'll go to college."

"I don't know. I guess I will. You're a dear sweet," exclaimed Stella sweetly.

Mark showed them out of the front door. Stella and her Mother left the house together. Mrs Avery and her emotional daughter got in a car. The parent drove her daughter, a passenger sitting on a passenger seat, home.

Mark standing by the doorway waved good-bye to them as they left. The parting was an emotional farewell!

8

Stella's Birthday

Mark popped in and gave Stella her birthday present and a belated birthday card. Mark received a warm welcome from guests. He been overwhelmed at the welcoming invitingness. He entered the dining room. All of the guests were females, Stella's friends.

Mark stood behind them gathering around. He watched Mrs Avery bring in a birthday cake and put it down on the dining table in front of her daughter seated at the dining table. Stella's face lit up. Her childish expression was girlish. Stella felt overwhelmed with excitement. Stella was filled with wonder and sheer delight. Stella leaned forward and blew out all of the lit candles on the birthday cake. She made a wish!

One of her friends put her hand on Stella's shoulder. Debbie rested her hand on her when leaning on her. A friend's loving gesture!

Mark experienced their deep love he witnessed. Her friends had such great love for Stella. Stella felt deeply emotional and affectionate. Stella was overwhelmed by all of her friends' deep love for her. She had great affection for them. Feeling love and affection for Stella. Stella's friends were all overwhelmed with such joy and bliss at being with their friend again!

Stella had tears of joy on her birthday. She felt deeply happy and blissful. She wished this great bliss and joy would last forever. She cherished it. Their promise of eternal friendship!

Stella wore on her finger a signet ring. It testified to that. It acted in a testimony to her promise!

Mark did not stay any longer at Stella's birthday party. He outstayed his welcome. Moving away from them. Standing around together. Seeing their expression of love. Their radiant beam.

Moving in the claustrophobic space. Mark slipped out of the dining room. Going out of the detached house. Mark got in his car parked in a front drive. There were other cars parked in the driveway. Mark drove home. He greatly missed Stella! He remained deeply emotionally attached to her. With deep sentimentality to his former school closed down. (Decades ago, a new Catholic secondary school college was established.)

9

Last Memory

At the weekend Mark's Mother came into the tidy lounge to do housework and spring clean.

From being intruded on Mark got up from the armchair. He stood up. He felt irritated and annoyed at his Mother's intrusion. Standing still Mark was restless and fidgety.

"Now that you are terminated. What are you going to do? What was your best thing that happened?" asked Mother.

Mark felt discomfort at standing too close to his Mother. He moved away from his Mother dusting a mantelpiece. His Mother was obsessed with cleanliness.

"Mom. I don't know," shrugged Son.

Mark thought deeply about it. From his experience, meeting "sexy" Stella remained the finest thing he ever experienced. Stella's schooldays were over!

10

Mark's Profound Vision

Mark had personal differences with his Mother. Consequently, Mark moved to another house. To keep his sanity. (From time to time he did stay at his Mother's house.)

His Mother rejected and neglected her son. His Mother deemed her son to be unfit for work.

One hot afternoon at his Mother's house, in his spare time Mark painted a picture on a canvas on an easel of a girl with golden hair. Using certain pastels and paints he painted. Her long hair was sandy – and gold too!

To Mark's satisfaction, he attained perfection. Mark was pleased with it. Finally completing it. Mark left the finished picture on an easel for weeks as an unveiled display.

Mrs Tomkins' friends and visitors came into her house and saw the mystique!

It was displayed with exotica and taxidermy. They had a mixed reaction and first impression. They admired the beautiful portrait.

Her natural countenance of a girl! With childlike innocence and a girlish and virgin's sweetness!

At the house individuals who saw it wondered who was the angelic mystique? With an angelic expression as well as natural look. The fair girl's beauty was admirable. Naturally the decent virgin was chaste. Her decency one of a virgin's!

Did an inspired Mark have inspiration and wonder? It was an object of inspirational motivation. Was it a vision? Was it a deep dream!

Mark's lost love for Stella was a deep love. A really great love. Mark fathomed a mystery. (A deep, profound and spiritual one!)

The Messiah with a child!

On one night standing alone by a portrait. He saw a country girl. An Angel whose hair was tied in pigtails. He thought it reminiscent of Stella. Her angelic countenance natural. It was something divine and pious. His deep memory lived on… It was typically evocative and heart-rending. His deep love for her burned. The portrait itself kindled his memory…

- THE END -

*Available worldwide from Amazon
and all good bookstores*

www.mtp.agency

www.facebook.com/mtp.agency

@mtp_agency

www.ingramcontent.com/pod-product-compliance
Lightning Source LLC
LaVergne TN
LVHW051218070526
838200LV00063B/4950